SUPER

Lori Ries
Illustrated by
Sue Ramá

SUPER

Lori Ries
Illustrated by
Sue Ramá

Special thanks to my family, Emily, and a little boy
I met in Chautauqua named Sam—L. R.

To all my amazing, wonderfully supportive brothers
and sisters. Thanks, my dears, for the blankie.
I am so grateful.—S. R.

Published by Charlesbridge
85 Main Street
Watertown, MA 02472
(617) 926-0329
www.charlesbridge.com

Library of Congress Cataloging-in-Publication Data
Ries, Lori.
    Super Sam!/ Lori Ries ; illustrated by Sue Ramá.
      p. cm.
    Summary: Sam transforms himself into Super Sam to entertain
his baby brother, but when his superpowers fail, he finds
another way to save the day.
    ISBN 1-58089-041-5 (reinforced for library use)
    [1. Brothers—Fiction. 2. Babies—Fiction.]
I. Ramá, Sue, ill. II. Title.
PZ7.R429Su   2004
[E]—dc22   2003015844

Printed in China
(hc) 10 9 8 7 6 5 4 3 2 1

Illustrations done in colored pencil,
    water-soluble crayon, and watercolor
Display and text type set in Lemonade
Color separations by Classic Scans
Printed and bound by Everbest Printing Company, Ltd.,
    through Four Colour Imports Ltd., Louisville, Kentucky
Production supervision by Brian G. Walker
Designed by Diane M. Earley

Sam.

SUPER SAM!

Run, **SUPER SAM!**

Fly, **SUPER SAM!**

Show your strength,

SUPER SAM!

Leap tall
buildings,

SUPER SAM!

Climb the cliff,
SUPER SAM!

Oh, no—a bear!

Become invisible,

SUPER SAM!

Escape,
SUPER SAM!

Save the day,
SUPER SAM!

Save the day, SUPER SAM!

Save the day,
SUPER SAM!

Sam?

Super, Sam.